WISHWORKS INC.

BY STEPHANIE S. TOLAN

ILLUSTRATED BY AMY JUNE BATES

SCHOLASTIC INC.
New York Toronto London Auckland
Sydney Mexico City New Delhi Hong Kong

ISBN: 978-0-545-22904-3

Text copyright © 2009 by Stephanie S. Tolan.
Illustrations copyright © 2009 by Amy June Bates.
All rights reserved. Published by Scholastic Inc.
SCHOLASTIC, the LANTERN LOGO, and associated logos are
trademarks and/or registered trademarks of Scholastic Inc.

Arthur A. Levine Books hardcover edition published by
Arthur A. Levine Books, an imprint of Scholastic Inc., June 2009.

12 11 10 9 8 7 6 5 4 3 2 1   10 11 12 13 14 15/0

Printed in the U.S.A.   40

First paperback printing, January 2010

For Maxwell Raymond Tolan,
who can visit Wishworks
any time he wants!
— S.T.

WISHWORKS
INC.

1 **IT WAS MAX'S SECOND DAY AT**
his new school. It was also the second day
the tall kid with the red buzz cut stood in
front of him in the hall and blocked the way to
his classroom. Two other boys stood a little
behind the buzz-cut kid so Max couldn't get
around him.

Yesterday, Max had tried to push his way
past. It hadn't worked. They had shoved him into
the wall. The rest of the day, his shoulder hurt.
Right now this minute if he touched the place,
it would still be sore. It wasn't fair. He wanted to
take them on, but there were three against one. If
only they would look away for a minute, maybe

he could dodge around them. "Look out!" he shouted, pointing over their heads. "He's going to get you!" Two of them turned to look where he was pointing, but the buzz-cut kid wasn't fooled.

He snatched Max's lunch box and ran for the boys' room. When Max started after him, the two others jumped in front of him. Max dodged sideways and they dodged with him. He dodged the other way and they did too. He pretended to dodge back, and when they moved to block him again, he got around them. But by that time, the buzz-cut kid was coming out of the boys' room with an evil grin on his face. His hands were empty.

Max found his lunch box in one of the toilets. He pulled it out and carried it, dripping, to the sink. He ran water over his lunch box and then washed his hands.

He wouldn't be able to eat his apple. His sandwich was in a ziplock bag. Ziplocks were supposed to keep water out. Even so, he knew he couldn't make himself eat the sandwich now. What made him maddest, though, was the butterscotch brownie his mother had let him take. It was the last one. Max had almost eaten it on the school bus. He wished now that he had. He opened his lunch box and emptied everything, even the brownie, into the trash.

Max looked into the mirror over the sink. His unhappy face looked back at him. "Only losers and wimps give in to bullies and their henchmen," his dad used to tell him. There had been bullies in his old school too. "You need to stand up for yourself. You need to give as good as you get."

Max made a ferocious face in the mirror. *I am not a loser,* he thought. *I am not a wimp.* He imagined a big, reddish-brown dog standing right behind him. The dog wagged his big plume of a tail. "Get him, King!" Max whispered. King bounded out into the hall and grabbed the buzz-cut kid's pants leg. The buzz-cut kid fell to the floor. In Max's mind, King jumped on the kid and stood with his front feet on his chest. King growled a deep, loud, scary growl. The buzz-cut kid howled. The kid's henchmen ran away.

Max saw himself walking calmly out of the boys' room and standing over the buzz-cut kid. "That's enough," he said to the dog. King came to sit beside him, a bit of blue denim between his teeth. The buzz-cut kid ran, crying, down the hall to the third-grade classroom. Max wiped his wet hands on his jacket. He patted King's head. No wimps or losers here.

The bell rang. Max left the boys' room and carried his still-dripping lunch box toward his classroom. He imagined King walking at his side, ears up, tail waving. "Good dog!" he whispered. Tomorrow he would not open his lunch box on the bus to see what was inside. He would keep it safely in his backpack. Inside the classroom, he put his jacket, his backpack, and the wet lunch box into his cubby and went to his seat. He imagined King lying down next to his feet, head and ears up, keeping watch.

When Mr. Malone, the third-grade teacher, took the roll, Max listened carefully. The buzz-cut kid's name was Nick Berger. He sat in the first row right in front of the teacher's desk. That was probably because Mr. Malone wanted to keep an eye on him. Nick's henchmen's names were Luis and Rocco. One sat in the middle of the room on the right. The other sat in the middle on the left. Mr. Malone must know about them. He was keeping them apart. Max was glad that the only seat left when he came to this school had been at the back of the room. He and King could keep an eye on all three of them.

All morning, Max stared at the back of Nick Berger's neck and imagined terrible things happening to him. First there was a red-and-purple dragon with fiery eyes that swooped down and picked Nick up with his huge claws. The dragon flew over a glowing volcano and dropped Nick in. Then there was a big, squinty-eyed man dressed all in black who shoved Nick into a cage made of iron bars. He put a heavy chain around the cage and a padlock on the chain. But best of all, Max thought, was when Nick opened his desk and scorpions swarmed out and ran up his arms.

"Do you know the answer, Max?" Mr. Malone asked at one point. Max had been so busy imagining a snake crawling up Nick's leg that he hadn't heard the question. He shook his head.

"No daydream- ing," Mr. Malone said. Max hated the word *daydream- ing*. His father

used to use it a lot. "Daydreaming will never get you anywhere," he would say.

"You need to pay attention," Mr. Malone said.

Max nodded. He tried to pay attention after that. But it was hard to care about the farm products of Mexico. Pretty soon he was imagining Luis and Rocco turning on Nick on the playground. They pulled his pants down. Under his pants, Nick was wearing pull-up diapers like the ones Max's sister, Polly, used to wear, with pink flowers. All the other third graders stood around Nick and laughed until he got loose from his henchmen and ran away. As he ran, Nick's face was redder than his buzz cut.

At lunchtime, Max sat by himself, keeping an eye on Nick and his henchmen. Thanks to them, he had nothing to eat. But that didn't mean they'd won. He imagined himself eating his favorite pizza. It had pepperoni and sausage, with mushrooms and extra cheese. When he took a bite, the cheese made long yellow strings that Max had to catch with his fingers. He shared the pizza with King, who wagged his tail with appreciation and licked Max's hand. Afterward, he imagined himself eating a huge butterscotch brownie and drinking a glass of ice-cold milk. He didn't share these with King. Brownies and milk weren't good for dogs.

When his stomach rumbled that afternoon, he ignored it. He told himself that he and King were spies in a school full of space aliens. It was a school that was teaching the aliens how to conquer Earth. He had to find out what they were learning so the governments of Earth could stop them. He was disguised to look just like the aliens, but their food was poisonous to humans. He dared not put a single bite of it into his mouth. A good spy didn't let hunger bother him.

The future of Earth depended on him.

2 "SO!" MOTHER SAID THAT EVE-
ning, while Max was helping himself to
more hamburger casserole. "How was
the second day in the new school?" Her forehead
was crinkled with concern. He'd heard her talking to Grandma on the phone and he knew she
was worried about them.

"Great!" his sister, Polly, said. "I made
another friend."

How did Polly do it? Max wondered gloom-
ily. Here they were in a whole different part of
the city, having to start a new school more than
halfway through the year, and already she had
two friends. Girls were probably easier to make
friends with than boys. Besides, Polly didn't have

to worry about bullies. If there was a kid like Nick Berger in Polly's first-grade class, he probably wouldn't pick on a girl.

Polly had cried the night they moved into this new house, which was really only the first floor of a house that was attached to other houses on both sides. It didn't even have a yard to play in, so she didn't have her swing or her sandbox anymore. Mother had held her in her lap and told her that she would get used to their new life. "There are good things here we didn't have in the old neighborhood." She reminded Polly that the park was only two blocks away and it had even more playground equipment than their old school's playground. "It'll be okay. You'll see."

And sure enough, by the end of the first day of school, Polly had been talking about her nice new teacher and a friend named Sophia.

Max told himself he didn't need friends. Other kids never wanted to do the things he liked to do. Besides, Adventure Time, his most favorite thing of all, he could do all by himself. He could have Adventure Time anywhere. Even here, in a house jammed right up against other houses.

"Max?" Mother asked. "How was your day?"

He hadn't mentioned Nick Berger and his henchmen yesterday. He didn't mention them now. He didn't want Mom worrying about him. "It was okay," he said. That wasn't even a lie. Not really. It had been fun imagining all those things happening to Nick Berger.

After dinner, Max helped with the dishes and sat at the table to write out the ten spelling words he had for homework. Then he went to his room. It didn't feel like his room. It was way smaller and not blue. It didn't have windows on two sides that looked out into a yard with trees that were just starting to get their new leaves.

The only window in this room looked out at the apartment house behind them. There was a draft that came in around the window even when it was closed. This room was chilly all the time.

Lots of his things were still in boxes. The boxes were stacked against the wall and on his bookshelves. He didn't even know what was in most of them. He should unpack them, his mother said, because having his belongings all around him would make the room feel more familiar, more like home. Max was afraid it would seem even less like home to see his old things in this new place.

The one thing that felt the same was his bed. His wizard sheets were on it, and the patchwork quilt of suns and moons and stars that Grandma had made. Now Ali Baba, the cat who had been a member of the family before Max and Polly, was curled up in the middle of his midnight-blue pillow, one paw over his nose. The fat gray cat was snoring gently. Ali Baba was one of the reasons Max could only have an imaginary dog. Ali Baba didn't like real ones.

If King were real, Max thought, Ali Baba could go sleep on Polly's bed instead of Max's. King would sleep with Max. He would stretch out right up against Max's back and keep him warm, even in this chilly room. And even if Max moved in the night and disturbed him, King would never put a claw into Max's foot the way Ali Baba did sometimes. Best of all, if King were real, he wouldn't be there only when Max was imagining him. He would be there all the time, always ready for adventure.

Max pushed Ali Baba off his pillow. The cat moved down the bed a little. In no time, he was snoring again.

Max pulled down his blind so he couldn't see the apartment building anymore. Then he fluffed his pillow and settled himself against it.

Polly had gone to bed and his mother was watching television. It was Adventure Time, the best time of the whole day.

Actually, Max thought, Adventure Time would be better in this new life than in the old one. Because here, Dad would never come barging in to ask what he was doing. He would never ever lecture Max about what he ought to do to be a *regular kid*.

Max didn't want to be a regular kid. He could tell from what they talked about at school that regular kids watched television before they went to bed. Or played video games. Some of them read books. All the stories on television or video games or in books were stories somebody else had made up. None of those stories could be his very own.

What Max did was much, much better. Here by himself on his bed, with nobody to interrupt him and nothing he was supposed to be doing instead, he could create whole worlds. He could go anywhere and do anything. There was nobody to tell him that imagination was childish and useless and a waste of time and to stop day-dreaming. There was nobody to tell him he needed to grow up and get real.

Max wasn't crazy about real. Real was a father who wanted him to be somebody he wasn't. Real was arguing and fighting and crying and divorce. And having to move. Right this minute, real was this room that didn't feel like his and a new school with kids he didn't know. Worse, real was Nick and his henchmen. And it was Mrs. Chang, who stayed with him and Polly after school and gave them only carrots or broccoli for snacks. And here, just like in the old house, real was boring old Ali Baba, who never did anything anymore except eat and sleep.

Max put his arms around his legs and rested his chin on his knees. He remembered the last adventure he and King had had together. They had started on the sidewalk outside the new house. There were lots of other people on the sidewalk, just like always, near the shops on 8th Avenue. All the people passing by had looked at Max and King with admiring glances. They were impressed by how beautiful King was and how well he behaved. Some of the people were walking dogs. There was a big black ferocious-looking dog that growled at King. King ignored it. His attention was focused on Max. There was a little white fluffy dog at the end of a jeweled leash, being walked by a woman in a frilly dress.

Suddenly, there had been a loud, rumbling sound and the sidewalk right in front of them cracked apart. Dust and smoke poured through the crack, and a huge green hairy monster climbed up and over the broken cement. The woman in the frilly dress screamed. People began to run. The monster reached out and snatched up the white fluffy dog in its claws. The little dog howled as the monster opened its jaws, showing long, sharp, jagged teeth. "Help, help!" yelled the woman. "It's going to eat Pookie!"

"Get him, King!" Max had shouted over the howls of the little dog. King jumped in front of the monster and began biting its toes. The monster hopped from foot to foot, yelping as it juggled the little dog in its claws. Max grabbed the end of the dog's jeweled leash and pulled. The little dog popped out of the monster's claws, and Max caught him as he fell. King kept biting the monster's toes as it backed toward the crack it had climbed out of. Max took the dog back to its grateful owner, who thanked him through her tears. "No problem," Max said. "My dog can do anything!"

It had been a very satisfying adventure. Now Max closed his eyes and felt himself getting very, very still. It was almost like disappearing. Sometimes he thought if Mom or Polly came into his room while he was off adventuring, they wouldn't be able to see him. It wasn't true, he knew. His father could always see him even if Max was adventuring clear off on another planet. But that's how it felt. It was as if he really, really went away into the story he was telling himself.

Sometimes Max planned ahead of time where he would go and the kind of adventure he would have. Other times he let the story create itself. Tonight he would just call King to go with him and see what happened. Whatever it was, it would be more fun than real life. Max thought about King and there King was, ears up, tail wagging. King was always ready for anything.

3 **MAX IMAGINED HIMSELF ON THE** sidewalk like the last time, heading toward the end of the block. Everything looked just the way it did in real life. Max didn't mind. It was Adventure Time. The sidewalk probably wouldn't crack open this time, but *something* would happen. He felt a little chill along the back of his neck, wondering what it would be. When they got to the corner, they turned left on 8th Avenue, and he saw something new. Right there on the corner where the Korean grocery store should have been, with its yellow awning and bins of vegetables and fruits on the sidewalk, there was a different shop entirely. It had a big window and a carved wooden door. Max smiled. The adventure was about to begin.

Above the window of the shop, in elegant gold letters, were the words WISHWORKS, INC. There were candies in the window. And kaleidoscopes. There were books and toy trains and rockets and stuffed animals. A hand-lettered sign leaned against a castle with turrets and pennants. WISHES, the sign said. GUARANTEED.

"Sit," Max told King. King sat. "Stay." King stayed on the sidewalk as Max pushed open the door to the shop.

A bell tinkled merrily. An old man with curly white hair and crinkly eyes was leaning against a wooden counter carved with trees and flowers and strange-looking animals unlike anything Max had ever seen before. The man was wearing a red-and-white checked apron. On the counter next to him was an old-fashioned cash register.

"Have you come to buy a wish?" the old man asked.

"What does the sign mean, 'guaranteed'?" Max asked.

"Just what it says. You buy a wish, it comes true. Guaranteed."

"You mean I *imagine* it comes true."

The old man shook his head. "I mean it comes true. For *real*."

Max looked around the shop. It was dim and shadowy. There were shelves from floor to ceiling, but there was nothing on them. The shop itself was empty except for the old man, the counter, and the cash register. It smelled old and dusty, as if it should be draped in cobwebs. As he thought that, cobwebs appeared in the dark corners.

Max thought about stuffed animals, and the shelves filled with stuffed animals. He thought about butterscotch brownies, and the shelves filled with trays of butterscotch brownies. The smell of them made Max's mouth water.

"But none of this is real," he said. "It's just a story I'm making up. I'm imagining this shop and what's on those shelves. I'm even imagining you."

The old man nodded, smiling. "Of course you are. Nevertheless — this is Wishworks, Inc. If you buy one of my wishes, it will come true. For real. Guaranteed."

"*Real* real?"

"As real as you are."

"How much does a wish cost?" Max asked. A real wish was valuable. It would probably be very, very expensive. He suspected he didn't have enough money to buy one.

"You always have what you need for a wish," the man said, as if he had heard Max's thought. "Check your pocket."

Max reached into his pocket and found, to his surprise, a twenty-dollar bill. That was more money than he had in his bank at home. He held it out.

"Exactly the price," the man said, and took it. He punched a key on the cash register and its drawer opened with a clang. He put the bill in and closed the drawer.

Max grinned. Even for twenty dollars, the wish would be a bargain. He would get a real wish for an imaginary twenty.

The man looked at Max, frowning so that his shaggy white eyebrows nearly met over his eyes. "This is the hard part. Think very carefully before you answer. Very carefully! What's your wish?"

Hard? Hard? It was the easiest thing in the world. Max didn't have to think at all. More times than he could remember, he had wished for a dog of his own. It was what he wanted more than anything else in the whole world. Max thought about King, sitting outside the shop, waiting for him. "I wish for a *real, live dog*," Max said.

There was a deep, chiming sound and the shop seemed to go dark for a second.

"Done!" said the old man.

Max looked around. The shelves were empty. The man leaning against the counter was still the only living thing in the shop except Max. No dog had appeared the way King always did when Max imagined him. He looked at the old man. "Well?"

The man smiled. "I meant your *wish* is done, of course, not the dog. The dog, being real, may take a little time."

"But it's guaranteed?"

The man nodded gravely. "Guaranteed!"

4 **KING WAS SITTING PATIENTLY**
on the sidewalk when Max came out of
the shop, the bell tinkling as the door
closed. The dog stood up, waving his long plume
of a tail. "Just you wait," Max told him, patting his
head. "Things are going to change. Guaranteed."

Maybe they had changed already, he thought.
Instead of imagining himself walking King
all the way back down the street toward home,
Max just took a deep breath and opened
his eyes.

His room looked exactly the way it had
before. Ali Baba was snoring softly. The boxes
labeled MAX'S THINGS were still stacked on his

shelves and against the wall. Max looked carefully around the room. There was no dog.

Max sighed. "The dog, being real, may take a little time," the old man had said. What did "a little time" mean? He got up from his bed and went out into the living room, where his mother was watching television.

Mother checked her watch and frowned. "It's late. I thought you'd gone to bed," she said.

"Not yet," Max answered. There was no dog in the living room.

How would the dog come? Max wondered. Maybe, he thought, a real dog had to come a regular, real way.

"Mom," he said, making his voice as sweet as he could manage, "do you think we could have a dog now that we've moved? In this neighborhood, it would be a good thing to have a watchdog, wouldn't it? It could be dangerous here. There are lots and lots of people around us all the time. Lots and lots of strangers."

His mother sighed. "This is a very nice neighborhood. Very safe. Think of all those people as friends we haven't met yet. Besides, you know perfectly well Ali Baba doesn't like dogs."

"Well, what if the dog liked Ali Baba?" Max said. "And what if I mostly kept him in my room? And what if he was a big, beautiful dog that always did what he was told? I'd take care of him. I promise! I'd walk him and feed him and —"

"No dog," Mother said, shaking her head. "Not even a paragon of perfection."

Max didn't need to know what *paragon* meant to understand that his mother wasn't going to help the real dog come into his life. He sighed and went back to his room.

How could his wish come true if his mother

wouldn't let it? *Guaranteed,* he reminded himself. The wish was guaranteed. Tonight, Mother was saying "No dog." Tomorrow might be different. Maybe that's why a real dog took time. There were real people involved. And real people, Max knew, could be difficult.

Max put on his pajamas, turned off his light, and snuggled down into his bed with Ali Baba curled against his legs. He thought about what his life would be like with a real dog. The real dog would be just like King. The real dog could even *be* King. He thought about how it would be to put his arm around King's big warm furry body and have him lick his nose.

Then Max had a terrible thought. What if, in spite of the guarantee, Mom could stop the wish from coming true? What if the guarantee only meant that if his wish didn't come true, he could get his money back? He didn't want that imaginary twenty-dollar bill. He wanted his dog!

He needed to go back to Wishworks, Inc. He needed to ask the old man some more questions. Max took a long, deep breath and imagined himself on the sidewalk outside the shop. It looked exactly the way it had looked before. In the window were the candies and kaleidoscopes, the books and toy trains and rockets and stuffed animals. And there was the sign leaning against the castle. WISHES GUARANTEED.

Inside, he could see the old man in his red-and-white checked apron, still leaning against the counter.

Max reached out to push open the door. But as he did, the door changed shape. It grew very, very tall. It turned to brick. There were lots and lots of windows. It had become the back wall of an apartment building. Then, before he even had a chance to wonder what had happened, the apartment building became a tree, its leaves just beginning to open.

Max had fallen asleep.

5 **WHEN MAX WOKE UP THE NEXT** morning, Ali Baba was still there and the dog still wasn't. He had to get up and get dressed for school. There was no time now to go back to Wishworks, Inc., no time to ask the old man about the guarantee. Maybe on the school bus.

At the breakfast table, he considered mentioning a big, beautiful, perfectly behaved dog again. But he didn't have the nerve. He didn't want to hear "no dog" even one more time. The more often his mother said it, the less likely she was to change her mind.

On the bus, Max tried to go to Wishworks, Inc. But Polly was sitting next to him, chattering on and on about her new friends. "Do you think Mom would let them come over after school sometime?" she asked. "Do you think Mrs. Chang would give them cookies?" She poked him. "I said, do you think Mom would . . ."

Max gave up.

At school Max scanned the school yard, looking for Nick and his henchmen before he would let Polly get off the bus. Maybe a first-grade bully wouldn't go after a girl, but he wasn't sure about Nick Berger. After a moment, he saw them standing around a very little boy up against the fence.

"Go find your friends," Max told Polly, but she was already waving at a cluster of first-grade girls. Max imagined King at his side as he walked close to a group of fifth graders, keeping them between him and Nick Berger. Between the shoulders of the older kids, Max saw the little boy hand Nick something. It looked like a package of chocolate cupcakes.

When the fifth graders met up with their friends, Max slipped around them and hurried up the steps to wait right by the door so that he would be the first one in when it opened. He got to his classroom before Nick and his henchmen, put away his things, and hurried to his desk, King beside him. "Down, King," he whispered under the noise of the other kids coming in. King lay down by his feet, his ears up, his eyes alert for danger. When Nick came in, shoving a couple of other kids out of his way, there was a smear of chocolate on his mouth.

During language arts, Nick went to sharpen his pencil at the back of the room and pulled Max's hair as he passed by. King could do nothing to stop him. Max imagined the pencil sharpener gobbling up Nick's pencil, then sucking in Nick's fingers and sharpening them too.

On the way outside to recess, Rocco came up behind Max and bumped him so hard he crashed into a wiry boy named Jerome. "Watch yourself, Rocco!" Jerome called after him. "Those guys are trolls," he said to Max. "Don't let them bother you."

Max nodded. Trolls — that's just what they were.

When the other boys started a game of dodgeball, Max didn't join in. But Nick threw a ball at him anyway, and hit him in the back of the head. Max imagined King biting the ball so that it went all flat and nobody could play with it again. But he also went and stood with his back to the one tree that grew up through the pavement on the playground. The truth was, having an imaginary dog for protection didn't make him feel that safe.

Max kept one eye on what Nick was doing

and one eye on the sidewalk outside the school's fence. It had been a lot more than a *little* time since he'd made his wish. Maybe the real dog would come walking down the sidewalk and into the playground. But no dog came.

When the bell rang to signal that recess was over, Max breathed a sigh of relief. Math was after recess. Max didn't have to pay attention to Mr. Malone talking about borrowing and carrying. He had had borrowing and carrying in his old school. Math was the perfect time to go back to Wishworks, Inc., and get his questions answered.

But when he got back to class, there was a policeman in the room with Mr. Malone. As soon as the kids came through the door, they all got very quiet. Everybody hurried to put their jackets away and sit in their seats. Max wondered if someone had called the police on Nick and his henchmen. As mean as they were, he didn't think they'd broken any actual laws.

"Class," Mr. Malone said when they were all in their places, "this is Officer Fisher, Jerome's father. He is our parent of the month and he's come to tell us all about his job."

For the next half hour, Max couldn't help paying attention. Everything Officer Fisher said was interesting. He told them he'd wanted to be a policeman since he was even younger than they were. He explained the training he had had to go through. One of the boys asked if he drove a police car. "I walk a beat," he said. "I like to stay close to what's going on in the neighborhood. I like to know the people I watch out for. I like to know who belongs there and who doesn't."

He told stories of the things that had happened while he was walking his beat. He had foiled a robbery at a jewelry store and arrested the robbers. He had found a lost toddler who had wandered away from his mother in a store. And when he saw bad guys hanging out where they didn't have any business, he moved them along.

Officer Fisher took his nightstick out of his belt and gave it to Mr. Malone to pass around the class. When Nick got it, he pretended he was going to hit Caitlin, the girl who sat next to him. Mr. Malone took it away from him and gave it to Caitlin instead. When the nightstick finally got around to Max in the back of the room, he was surprised at how heavy it was. He could knock out a goblin or even a giant with a nightstick like this. He thought he would take one with him during Adventure Time that night, just in case. Officer Fisher showed them his gun too, but he didn't let them touch that.

When Officer Fisher finished answering all their questions, he told them they should consider joining the force when they grew up. Mr. Malone thanked him for coming and the class applauded. As he was about to leave, Officer Fisher looked at Caitlin, then at Nick

Berger, then back to Caitlin. "If you became a police officer," he said to her, "you could protect people from anyone who thinks it's okay to hurt other people."

Max wondered if Jerome had told his father about Nick and his henchmen. The other kids laughed. Nick's ears got very red.

Jerome Fisher was just about the luckiest boy in the world, Max thought. His father was a real person who had real adventures and did noble deeds every single day. No wonder Jerome could yell at Rocco. And no wonder, even though Jerome wasn't any bigger than Max was, he could say not to let Nick and his henchmen bother him. A real policeman father was much better protection than an imaginary dog.

When Mr. Malone announced after lunch that it was time to catch up on the math they'd missed in the morning, everyone groaned except Max. Finally he would be able to go to Wishworks,

Inc., and find out what was going on with his wish. He set his book up on his desk to provide some cover and closed his eyes. Immediately he was back on the sidewalk outside the shop. As he opened the door, the bell tinkled and the old man behind the counter looked up. He smiled when he saw it was Max. Max didn't smile back.

"You said a real dog would take a little time. How long?" he asked.

"As long as necessary," the old man said.

"Do you mean I might not get my dog till I'm all grown up?"

The old man's smile faded. "Do you think that will be just a *little* time?"

Max shook his head. "That will be a long time."

The smile came back. "Well, then! There's your answer."

"Is the guarantee only a money-back guarantee?"

The old man laughed and shook his head. "What good would it do you to have imaginary money instead of a real dog? No, no. Our guarantee is just what it says. A wish you buy from Wishworks, Inc., is guaranteed to come true."

Now Max smiled. All he needed to do was wait a little longer, he thought.

"Max!" Mr. Malone's sharp voice brought Max back to the classroom. "I asked if you can take eight from six!"

Max looked at the problem Mr. Malone was pointing to on the whiteboard at the front of the room. There was a thirty-six with an eight below it and a line underneath. Thirty-six minus eight. Easy. "You can take eight from six," Max said, "if you borrow from the tens column."

Mr. Malone, looking surprised, nodded. "Can you come up here and show us?"

Max went to the front of the room, stepping carefully over the foot Nick shot out to trip him. He took the marker Mr. Malone held out. He crossed out the three in thirty-six and wrote a two above it. "When you borrow from the tens column, the three becomes a two and the six becomes sixteen," Max said and wrote a one squeezed in beside the six. "Sixteen minus eight is eight." He wrote an eight under the line. "There's nothing to subtract from the two, so you just bring it down." He wrote a two beside the eight and handed the marker back to Mr. Malone. "The answer is twenty-eight."

"Very *good*, Max!" Mr. Malone said.

Max started back to his seat. "I apologize," Mr. Malone said. "I thought you were daydreaming again."

Max ducked the rubber band Luis shot at him and shook his head. Whatever Wishworks, Inc., was, he felt sure it wasn't a daydream.

6 MAX OPENED HIS EYES. HE WAS in bed with Ali Baba on his legs. A tiny sliver of gray light was visible along the edge of his window shade. Was that the doorbell he had heard? Who could be ringing their doorbell so early? It wasn't even time to get up and get ready for school.

He heard his mother hurrying down the hall and unlocking the front door. Then he heard voices. He moved Ali Baba and got up. He went out to the living room in his pajamas. Ali Baba followed him.

Beyond his mother he could see a baseball cap with long gray hair sticking out. It was Mrs. Kavitsky, the woman who lived upstairs, whose front door was right next to theirs and shared the same stoop. She and his mother were both talking at once. "We can't," his mother was saying. "We have a cat — an old cat —"

"I was out doing my morning run, and this poor thing came tearing across 17th Street. She was nearly hit by a car. You can tell nobody has been taking care of her. Who knows how long she's been on her own."

Max saw now what they were talking about. It was shivering in Mrs. Kavitsky's arms. It was a dirty yellow color and only a little bigger than a loaf of bread. Odd tufts of hair sprouted around its ears. Its legs were short and skinny. They clawed at Mrs. Kavitsky's sweatshirt.

There was no doubt about it. The thing was a dog. *A real, live dog.* Max caught sight of the creature's rear end. Instead of a lovely plume, there was a long, thin, almost naked tail that reminded him of a rat.

No, no, no! This wasn't anything at all like King. There was some mistake. This was most certainly *not* the dog he had wished for.

Mrs. Kavitsky, holding the quivering rat-tailed dog, stepped inside. His mother was still shaking her head. "We can't. We just can't," she said.

Max breathed a sigh of relief. Of course she wouldn't take it. He was pretty sure if his mother could just see King, just meet him once, Max could persuade her to let him keep him. But nobody could want this horrible little rat-tailed dog.

Mrs. Kavitsky's eyes filled with tears. "I guess I'll have to take her to the pound, then. I was going to keep her myself, but when I took her upstairs, my Schatzi went after her and chased her three times around the apartment.

Females often don't get along, you know. Schatzi scared her half to death. Just look how the poor little thing is shaking."

"You're going to take her to the pound?" Mother said in a very small voice.

Mrs. Kavitsky nodded, tears beginning to trickle down her pink cheeks. "Let's face it, this dog is no beauty. She isn't likely to get adopted. You know what will happen to her at the pound."

Mother looked hard at the shivering dog in Mrs. Kavitsky's arms. Mother's forehead was all wrinkled, and Max thought she looked as if she might be about to cry too.

Just then, Polly came down the hall from her room in her pink-and-white polka-dot nightgown. "Why is everybody up so early?"

Before anyone could answer, she saw the dog in Mrs. Kavitsky's arms. "Oooooh," she squealed, "what a cute little doggie!"

Polly must be blind, Max thought.

"Can we keep him?" Polly asked.

No! Max thought.

"Her," Mrs. Kavitsky said. "It's a sweet little girl dog."

"Awwww! Can we keep her? Can we? Can we?" Polly said, and started tugging at their mother's robe.

Max wished he could think of some way to shut Polly up. But it was too late. His mother's forehead wasn't wrinkled anymore. He could absolutely *see* her changing her mind.

"Oh, all right," Mother said then. "I guess we could take her. Max has always wanted a dog."

Mrs. Kavitsky beamed. "Wonderful! Just wonderful! Every boy should have a dog." As she bent to put the dog on the floor, it stiffened. It barked. Or yipped. Or maybe yapped. Whatever it was, the sound was bigger than the dog itself, Max thought. Its eyes were fixed on something behind Max. Max turned around to see. Ali Baba was pressed against the living room wall. His

back was arched. His tail was puffed up to twice its regular size. Ali Baba hissed.

The dog squirmed out of Mrs. Kavitsky's grasp. A streak of dirty yellow flew past Max's legs. Ali Baba hissed again and flashed out a paw full of claws. There was a yip that turned into a yelp. Then Ali Baba ran. He moved faster than Max had ever seen him move. He went under the couch. The dog, with a long red scratch on its muzzle, tried to go after him. It got stuck halfway and stayed there, its long, ratty tail wagging wildly. From under the couch came hisses and little high-pitched whines.

"Looks like Ali Baba can take care of himself," Mother said.

"OKAY, MAX," MOTHER SAID AS soon as Mrs. Kavitsky left. "You've got your dog. I'll pick up all the things we'll need for her on my way home from work tonight. But she's absolutely disgustingly dirty." She checked her watch. "There's just time before school for you to give her a bath."

"A bath? I've never given a dog a bath —"

"It isn't hard. Water in tub, dog in tub, wash dog, rinse dog, dry it with towels. I'll get you some old ones. And you can use Polly's no-tears shampoo. You said if you could have a dog, you'd take care of it."

Max had to drag the ratty little dog out from under the couch three times. As soon as he let her go, she would run right back after Ali Baba and get stuck again. Finally he had to carry her, wriggling and whining, into the bathroom and shut the door. As he ran water in the tub, the dog scratched and whined to get out and chase Ali Baba.

Then, when he put her into the tub, she struggled and splashed and tried to climb out. She scratched Max's arms with her sharp little claws. She didn't like getting a bath.

"Tough," Max told her. "I don't like giving you a bath either!" By the time Max was finished, he was as wet as the dog. When he tried to dry her, the dog grabbed a corner of the towel in her teeth and started tugging. Max was surprised at how strong she was. He couldn't get the towel away from her, even though her claws slipped on the wet tile floor. He dragged the dog around the bathroom until finally the corner of the towel tore completely off. This real, live dog had very sharp teeth.

Even clean, the dog was ugly. Really, really ugly, Max thought. Polly didn't think so. Polly thought the dog was cuter than ever. Mother said the dog was a lovely color. She also said they should name her quickly so she could get used to her name. Polly wanted to call the dog Cuddles. Max suggested Ratty. Mother didn't listen to either of them. She named the dog Goldie.

Max decided he would stick with Ratty anyway.

When it was time to leave for school, Mother said, "It seems as if Ali Baba can hold his own with this dog. But until they get used to each other, we probably shouldn't leave them alone together. She's yours, Max. When we aren't here, she'll have to stay in your room."

So Max dragged the still-damp dog back out from under the couch. "Sit and stay, Ratty," he said as he closed his door. But he could hear that she wasn't sitting. Or staying.

When they got to the bus stop, Polly was still talking about their new dog. Max wanted her to quit. He wanted to forget how badly his wish had turned out. Jerome Fisher was one of the kids waiting for the school bus, he noticed. He must live nearby. He and Max were the only third graders who got on at this stop. When Jerome got onto the bus, he sat near the back by himself. Max would have liked to sit with him instead of Polly. He wanted to ask what it was like having a policeman for a father. But Mother had said he had to sit with Polly till she had friends of her own to sit with.

"Isn't she the most beautiful dog you ever saw?" Polly asked him as he sat down next to her. "Aren't you glad you finally got a dog of your very own? Will you let me feed her and walk her sometimes? Will you, will you?"

"Any time," Max said. "Any old time."

All morning, Max had trouble paying attention in class. All he could think about was his wish and the horrible little rat dog. Mr. Malone accused him of daydreaming two different times.

At lunch, Nick Berger sat down next to Max. Luis sat on the other side of him and Rocco stood behind him. "Give me that bag of potato chips," Nick said. He already had a bag of chips they'd taken from a second grader and a pudding cup from Caitlin.

Max gave him the bag of chips, and the three of them went off to share their loot. Max didn't care. There were worse things in life than losing a bag of potato chips. Jerome was sitting at the next table. He threw Max a half-empty bag of pretzels and mouthed the word *trolls*. Max grinned and nodded.

On the bus ride home, Polly went right back to talking about the dog. Max slumped in his

seat and put his hands over his ears. He thought and thought about his guaranteed wish. He remembered the exact words he'd used when he made it. *A real, live dog.* Clearly, his wish had come true. Ratty was a dog. She was alive. And she was certainly real. The scratches on his arms proved that! But she wasn't the dog he wanted. It was King he'd been thinking about when he made his wish. The man at Wishworks, Inc., should have known that! King had been sitting right there on the sidewalk outside the shop at the time. What good was a guaranteed wish if it didn't match what you were thinking about when you made it? It had all gone awfully, horribly, dreadfully wrong.

8 WHEN MAX GOT HOME FROM
school, he found that Ratty had chewed
the ears off his old teddy bear and made
a puddle on the floor of his closet. Mother came
home early from work, bringing a red collar and
matching leash, a ball, a rawhide chew toy, and a
bag of dog food.

"It isn't her fault," she said when he complained about the puddle in his closet. "I should
have had you take her out before we left. From
now on, you're going to have to walk her every
morning until she's finished doing her

business, and then again as soon as you come home from school," she told him. "And there's a pooper-scooper law, so you'll have to take a trowel and a plastic bag along with you."

"You mean I have to pick up her poop and bring it home?"

"You can put it in the nearest trash can. I'll walk her one last time every night before I go to bed."

From then on, Max was in charge of the dog. He had to get up half an hour early to walk her before school. He carried the trowel and the plastic bag for Ratty's poop in a grocery bag. It was embarrassing. At first he tried to make believe it was King he was walking. But it didn't work. Ratty was nothing at all like King.

Even with a leash, Ratty didn't walk nicely at his side. She dragged him first one way and then another. She was little, but she was all muscle.

And he very quickly learned that Ratty didn't like to chase just Ali Baba. She liked to chase anything that ran. Outside, that was mostly squirrels. If she saw a squirrel across the street, Max had to grab hold of a lamppost or wedge himself against a parked car to keep from being pulled into traffic.

Sometimes while they walked, he tried to pretend he was a spy. There were lots of people walking their dogs every morning. A spy might walk a dog to blend in so whoever he was spying on wouldn't notice him. But a spy would never have a dog like Ratty. Everybody noticed Ratty. She barked — a lot. She barked at other dogs. She barked at pigeons. She barked at people carrying anything that smelled like food, and she tried to jump up on them to get it.

People frowned at her and shook their heads. They frowned at Max. He had to spend half their walks apologizing to strangers. But by the third day, some of them weren't strangers anymore. They knew Ratty and they knew Max. They waved newspapers or shook briefcases at them to keep them away. Some of them took to crossing the street to avoid them.

The worst part of their walk was passing LaRosa's Italian Grocery and Wine Shop. Ratty whined and yelped and jumped at the window, where cheeses of all shapes and sizes and piles of sausages were displayed. She seemed to be able to smell them through the glass. It was all Max could do to drag her away. A big man with a thick, black mustache came to the window and shook his huge fist at them sometimes.

There was one little old lady they saw every morning, though, who seemed to like the dog. Max thought she might be crazy. She carried little bone-shaped biscuits in her pockets and would dig some out as soon as she saw them coming. She would stop in front of them on the sidewalk. "Sit!" she would say to Ratty in a high, thin voice. Ratty made her skinny rattail go around and around in circles, but she never sat. The woman threw her three biscuits anyway, one at a time. Ratty would catch them right out of the air. Max had to give the dog a little credit for that at least. She never missed. *"Good dog!"* the woman always said. "She's smart enough," she added one day. "You should take her to obedience school."

Max just nodded. *King would never have to go to obedience school,* he thought.

At home Ratty chased Ali Baba. Yapping gleefully, she chased him down the hall. She chased him around the kitchen. She chased him under the chairs and the couch. When he came out, she chased him onto and over the couch, scattering pillows. She chased him into Polly's room and out again. She chased him right over Mrs. Chang while she was watching her TV talk show. Mrs. Chang didn't get mad. She thought it was funny.

Whenever Max poured dog food into her bowl, Ratty heard the sound and came as fast as she could, her claws skidding on the kitchen tiles. Her skinny rattail went around and around. She yipped with excitement and jumped all over him. Sometimes she nearly knocked the bowl out of his hands before he could put it on the floor.

"Why can't Polly feed her sometimes?" he asked Mother. "Why can't Polly walk her?"

"Polly's too little," Mother said.

She was right, Max thought with a sigh. Polly could never handle Ratty. It was all he could do to handle her himself. Ratty was probably the worst dog in the whole entire world.

Nobody else agreed with him. Polly thought she was adorable. Whenever Polly called her, the dog would flop down on the floor and beg for a tummy rub. Ratty loved it when Polly rubbed her tummy. Polly dressed her in doll clothes and tried to get her to ride in a stroller. When Ratty jumped out of the stroller and pulled the doll clothes off with her teeth, Polly only laughed and rubbed her tummy some more. Then Ratty would jump up and lick Polly on the nose, waggling all over. The dog looked particularly ugly when she was waggling all over, Max thought.

Mother liked the dog almost as much as Polly did. She let Ratty sit on the couch while she was reading and even shared peanuts with her. Ratty caught the peanuts in midair too.

Max told Mother that Ratty chased the cat too much. "Ali Baba could have a heart attack," he warned.

"I doubt it," Mother said. "This morning I saw Ali Baba lying in wait behind the couch. He pounced on her when Goldie went by. After that, you couldn't tell who was chasing whom. I haven't seen him this active since he was a kitten. I think he may be losing weight. Goldie's good for me too. I get exercise walking her every night. Who knew that we *all* wanted a dog?"

They were all crazy, Max thought.

And Ratty chewed. She chewed on her rawhide toy, of course, but that wasn't all. She chewed on the corners of the boxes in Max's room. Once when he came home, she had chewed clear through the cardboard on one of them and pulled out his favorite knight action figure. Then she had chewed his head off. Max began unpacking the boxes so he could put his things up on his shelves where they would be safe.

One day a second-grade girl asked Polly to sit with her. So Max went to the back of the bus and sat down beside Jerome Fisher. "Hi," he said. "Is it okay if I sit here?"

"Sure."

Max didn't know what else to say. A scuffle started between some older kids, and the bus driver yelled at them. "They wouldn't do that if your father was on the bus."

"No," Jerome said.

"It must be great to have a policeman for a father," Max said.

"It's okay," Jerome said. "But Mom worries about him a lot."

"Oh."

"I tell her he's a hero and nobody has to worry about heroes. What does your dad do?"

"He's a salesman," Max said. Nobody had ever heard of a hero salesman, he thought. "He lives in Chicago."

"Oh. Is that dog I saw you walking one day yours?"

Rats! Max thought. He had hoped nobody from school would ever see him with Ratty. He shook his head. "I was just walking her for the family she lives with."

"I've always wanted a dog," Jerome said. "For as long as I can remember."

"Can't you have one?" Max asked.

Jerome shook his head. "No way. My mom's allergic. The only pet I can have is a goldfish. His name is Sam. He's boring."

Max nodded. "My mom likes dogs." *At least,* he thought, *she likes one dog.* And then, before he could stop himself, he heard himself saying, "I have a big dog with a plume of a tail. His name is King."

"You're lucky," Jerome said.

"Yeah."

Why, Max wondered later, had he lied? What if Jerome saw him walking Ratty again — and again? And what if he wanted to know why he never saw him walking King? Max couldn't very well tell him that even if he *was* walking King, Jerome wouldn't be able to see him. It was all Ratty's fault, Max thought. If she wasn't in his life, he wouldn't have had to lie.

But the very worst thing about Ratty was what she did to Adventure Time. After dinner and homework, when Max settled on his bed to make up his stories, Ratty jumped up too. She climbed into his lap and licked his face. She had terrible breath. He had to wipe his face on his pillowcase to get her spit off him.

As soon as he closed his eyes and started to get quiet, Ratty would claw at his arms to get his attention. Before he could even start imagining a story, she would drop her ball in his lap. Then she would jump down off the bed and yip and yip until he threw it for her. No matter how hard he threw it or how high it bounced, Ratty could jump up and snatch it out of the air. If somehow she missed and it went under his dresser, she

whined till he got up and dug it out for her. By the time she was tired of playing and would leave him alone, Max was too sleepy to stay awake long enough for an adventure.

Max looked forward to school every day. There was no Ratty at school. Max could have King with him instead. It was taking a long time for the rest of the class to learn borrowing and carrying, so during math,

Max and King could go up in the space shuttle. They could conquer invading armies of goblins. They could hunt tigers in the jungle or terrorists in the city. They could save little kids who fell into fast-running streams, and get medals for bravery.

Nick stole Max's homework from his cubby one day. But he only hid it. He didn't chew it all up and leave slimy wet bits of it all over the floor. When Rocco or Luis bumped into Max in the hall or crashed into him on the playground, they didn't leave claw scratches on his arms and legs.

One night, Max woke up shivering. He had tried to make Ratty sleep on the floor, but she liked his bed better. He remembered how he had wanted King to sleep on his bed, the way Ali Baba used to, to keep him warm with his long, dog body. But Ratty had turned around and around and around and scratched at his quilt until she made herself a comfortable nest. Max was left with nothing but the sheet. Ratty's head was draped across his arm. His hand had fallen asleep and he couldn't feel his fingers. *Something,* he thought, *has to be done.*

WHEN MAX WAS WALKING RATTY after school the next day, he saw Jerome on the sidewalk across the street. He hoped Jerome wouldn't look his way. He didn't want him to see him walking Ratty again. He didn't want Jerome to ask about King.

A bus went by, hiding Max and Ratty from Jerome for a moment. Hurriedly, Max dodged into the nearest shop, dragging the dog with him through the door and closing it behind them. Jerome wouldn't be able to see them now. But no sooner had the door closed than Ratty began to yip and strain at her leash, standing on her back legs and dancing around like a circus dog. Max looked to see what had gotten into her. Too late, he realized he had brought her into LaRosa's. Ratty was struggling to reach the window display of sausages and cheese.

She had gone from yipping now to howling. It was a sound she'd never made before, so strange and loud it made goose bumps rise on his arms. Max jerked on the leash to make her stop. She just howled louder and dragged him sideways toward the window.

"Out!" a voice yelled from the back of the shop, so loud that it nearly drowned out Ratty's howling. "Out, out, out!" From behind a meat display case came the man with the black mustache. He was much worse than a troll or a giant. His white apron was stained with blood, and he held aloft a gleaming silver meat cleaver. His face was nearly as red as the stains on his apron. Max desperately tried to drag Ratty back to the door, but Ratty was pulling too hard toward the sausages in the window.

A woman with bright red lipstick, pushing a small shopping cart filled with bottles of wine, was blocking the narrow aisle between the man and Max. "You shouldn't have a dog in here," the woman said. "I'm sure there's a law!"

"Out!" the man yelled again, waving the cleaver wildly. He stormed around a stack of cans and started down the shop's other narrow aisle. There was nothing to stop him now, Max thought. He would be on them in no time. Ratty was pawing at a pyramid of wine bottles in front of the window, trying to climb it to reach the sausages. Max pulled on her leash with all his might. Ratty and the whole pyramid of bottles came crashing down.

Wine bottles rolled in every direction. The woman screamed, the man shouted something in a language Max didn't understand, and Max

lost his hold on the leash. Bounding over the rolling bottles, Ratty leaped into the window, grabbed a sausage between her teeth, jumped back down, and ran for the door. Max scrambled after her.

"You should do something about that dog!" the woman said. Max managed to get hold of the end of the leash as the man was still stumbling among the bottles. Max shoved open the door and he and Ratty, sausage firmly between her jaws, burst out onto the sidewalk. The sound of the man's voice, shouting more words he didn't understand, followed him out.

He *would* do something about Ratty, Max thought as he ran down the sidewalk toward home. And he knew what that something would be! When they'd turned the corner, he slowed down. Ratty had somehow managed to run and gulp down the sausage at the same time. *She must have swallowed it whole,* he thought. He half expected to hear pounding footsteps behind him, to have Jerome Fisher's father chase him down and arrest him for theft.

"We're going home right now," he told Ratty. "And you'd better do your business before we get there. Because I'm not taking you out again!"

When he let himself and Ratty into their house, Mrs. Chang was watching her talk show. Polly was at the table pretending to feed broccoli to her doll. Max put away the trowel and the poop bag. He hadn't had to use them. As soon as he took off her leash, Ratty chased Ali Baba under the couch.

"Take care of the dog," Max told Polly. "I have something important to do."

"Okay," Polly said. "You want a broccoli?" she asked Ratty.

"Dogs don't eat broccoli," Max said.

Ratty, her tail wagging, came and put her front paws on Polly's leg. Polly held out a piece of broccoli. Ratty took it. "This dog does," Polly said. Ratty crunched the broccoli, swallowed it down, and wagged for another.

King wouldn't eat broccoli, Max thought as he went to his room. *And he wouldn't steal sausages!* He closed his door to keep Ratty out. Then he settled himself on his bed. He took a deep breath and got quiet.

He didn't bother imagining the sidewalk or the door. He just imagined himself standing in front of the counter at Wishworks, Inc. The old man looked startled at Max's sudden appearance. Then he smiled. "Welcome back," he said. "What can I do for you?"

"I need customer service," Max said. "I need refunds and exchanges."

The old man frowned. "Am I to understand you are dissatisfied?"

"Yes, I'm dissatisfied!" Max said. He explained that when he made his wish, he had wanted King, not Ratty.

"Ah," the old man said, pressing the finger-tips of one hand to his chin. "But I understood that you wanted a *real* dog."

"I did. But I wanted King to be real!"

The old man sighed. "That's different, you know. It isn't what you wished. I warned you to think very carefully before you made your wish. I'm afraid we don't do refunds or exchanges. Once a wish becomes real, you can't return it. You can't trade it in for something else. Real is real."

"But that dog is messing up my whole life! Can't you do *anything*?"

The old man ran a hand through his curly white hair. "What could I do? You're just imagining me, remember."

This wasn't going at all the way Max had expected.

"*You* can do something, though," the man said. "You can buy another wish."

Max grinned. Of course! He should have thought of that himself. He reached into his pocket. He found another twenty-dollar bill and handed it over.

The old man took it and put it in the cash register drawer. "Make your wish. But this time, think *very, very carefully*."

Max had no need to think at all. "I wish Ratty would go away!" he said.

There was a deep chiming sound, and the shop went dark momentarily.

"Done," the old man said.

10 **MAX OPENED HIS EYES. IF**
this wish took as long as the other
one to come true, he would have to
put up with Ratty for a while yet. He saw that
he'd left his backpack on the floor. He got up and
hung it on a hook in his closet so Ratty couldn't
get at it and chew its straps again.

He could hear Mrs. Chang's television program droning from the living room. *Polly must
have taken the dog to her room,* Max thought. He
hoped he could leave his room now without
Ratty jumping on him and demanding that he
play with her. He didn't want to see Ratty again.
He didn't want to think about LaRosa's and the
big man with the meat cleaver. But he couldn't

help it. Even though Max didn't know the words he had shouted, the man's voice seemed to be stuck inside his mind. Maybe he could take money from his bank and pay for the sausage Ratty had stolen. He opened his door carefully and looked out into the hall.

Just then, Max heard the front door slam. "Max! Max! Help!" Polly hollered. "Come quick! Come now!" She came running down the hall toward him, Ratty's leash dragging on the floor behind her. At the end of the leash was Ratty's red collar with no Ratty. Polly's face was streaked with tears. "Goldie's gone! She's gone! You gotta help me find her!"

That was fast, Max thought. Had the dog just vanished — *poof!* — the moment he'd wished her away? Polly grabbed his hand. She was crying and pulling at him. He wanted to shout and cheer for the magic of it all, but it didn't seem right with Polly crying like that.

Mrs. Chang came hurrying from the living room. "What's wrong? What happened?"

Between sobs, Polly managed to tell them that Goldie had scratched and whined at the door till Polly went to get her leash. "You didn't hardly walk her at all!" she told Max. "She still had to go!" She sniffled and snuffled and explained to Mrs. Chang that Max had told her to take care of the dog because he had something important to do. "So I took her out myself."

"You should have called me," Mrs. Chang told her. "I would walk her with you."

"You were watching your program. And Max said I should take care of her!" Polly had clipped the leash to Goldie's collar, she told them. Then she had gotten the poop bag and trowel. "I did everything just the way Max does," she said. "And it was all okay. It was! Till Goldie saw a squirrel. She started barking and pulling and I

could hardly hold her. Then all of a sudden she sort of ducked her head, and her collar came right off over her ears. She chased the squirrel under some bushes and I didn't see her anymore. She was just gone. I yelled and yelled for her, but she didn't come back! She's gone, she's gone, she's gone, and it's all my fault!" Polly wailed.

It made Max's chest hurt to see Polly's face all red and crumpled and sad. *She'll get over it,* Max told himself. Ratty was the only dog Polly had ever known. She had no way of knowing what a terrible dog Ratty was. She didn't understand how a dog was supposed to be. Ratty had been with them only a few weeks. It wasn't as if she'd had the dog her whole life.

"We must go out," Mrs. Chang said. "We must find the dog before something bad happens. We must find the dog before your mother comes home."

Max thought about Wishworks, Inc. He thought about wishes that were guaranteed. Even with all three of them looking, they would not find Ratty, he thought. But he couldn't very well tell them that.

So Max went outside with Polly and Mrs. Chang to look for the dog. Mrs. Chang took Polly with her across the street and told Max to go left on 8th Avenue. He would go past the Korean grocery and the antique shop and the deli, but he'd turn back before he got to LaRosa's. "Goldie! Goldie!" Polly and Mrs. Chang called as they walked.

Max didn't call for the dog. He asked a couple of people he passed if they had seen a scruffy little yellow dog with no collar. Nobody had. Of course not. *I wish Ratty would go away* is what he had said. And she'd gone.

Polly will feel better in a day or two, he thought. He was sure of it. It wasn't bad like divorce. Or their father moving to another state and not even calling them a single time. Their lives would just go back to the way they were before he'd wished Ratty into them. He hadn't thought their lives were very good then, but he knew better now.

11 WHEN MOTHER CAME HOME, Polly was in her room, crying. Mrs. Chang explained what had happened. Mother took the collar and leash and went out to search for the dog. When she came back, there were frown lines between her eyes, and her mouth was turned down. Her eyes looked red as if she might have been crying too. She looked the way she used to look a lot of the time in the bad old days before the divorce. Max realized that he hadn't seen her like that a single time since they moved. That thought also made his chest hurt. He reminded himself what a good thing it was

90

that Ratty wasn't here anymore. It didn't help very much.

"I'm afraid she's really gone," Mother said. "We'll put up signs. And we can run an ad."

Max helped make signs that said LOST DOG. Mother put their phone number and address on the signs. But Max knew nobody would call. And nobody would bring Ratty back. His wish was guaranteed. Mrs. Chang took the signs and a big roll of tape so she could put them up around the neighborhood on her way home. "I miss that little dog already," she said as she left.

Mother made macaroni and cheese for supper. She said they all needed comfort food. Even though it was her favorite meal in the whole world, Polly hardly ate any. It was Max's favorite too. Like always, he asked for a second helping. Every night while they ate supper, Polly talked about her friends and her day at school. Not tonight. And Mother didn't ask any questions either. The whole meal was very quiet except for Polly's sniffling. She had to keep wiping her nose with her napkin.

Polly shouldn't be such a baby, Max thought. She wasn't a kindergartner anymore. And besides, Ratty was only a horrible little dog. But sitting there between his sniffling sister and his quiet mother, Max didn't feel like finishing his macaroni and cheese.

Later, when he was helping to clear the table, Max noticed Ratty's food and water bowls on the floor. He picked them up and put them in the dishwasher. Ratty didn't need them anymore. *Where did a dog go when it got wished away?* he wondered. She was a real dog when she was with them. Was she still real now? If she was still real, he supposed she still needed to eat. Probably she had found somebody else to feed her, somebody else to jump on and scratch when they tried to put her food on the floor. Max hoped she had found somebody. But he felt sorry for whoever she had found.

He did his homework at the table without being reminded. He had to copy ten spelling words and do five easy borrowing and carrying problems. When he was finished, he went to his room. Ratty's ball was on his pillow. He pushed it off onto the floor and settled himself on his bed. The ball bounced a couple of times and rolled under his desk. There was no Ratty to go under there and get it. There was no Ratty to drop it in his lap and then bark and yap at him till he threw it. *Good.* Ratty wouldn't be there ever again to jump up and snatch balls out of the air. *Very good!*

There was nothing at all to keep him from Adventure Time now, he thought. That was the best thing of all. It would be the first big adventure he and King had had since Ratty invaded his life.

He closed his eyes and got quiet. Then he

imagined himself at the edge of a forest, a big, grassy meadow stretching away toward a very high mountain with snow on the top. King was there, standing in front of him, wagging his tail. "Let's go," Max said, and set off across the meadow. King trotted next to him. Sometimes King would run ahead a little and make a big circle around him as if checking for danger, and then come panting back, his tongue hanging out.

Suddenly a cloud seemed to pass over the sun. It made a big shadow on the grass. Max looked up. It was no cloud. A huge dark shape with wings like a bat was swooping down at him. It was too big to be a bat or a bird and too nearly round to be a dragon. It was hard to see clearly against the brightness of the sky. Whatever it was, it wasn't friendly. King had gone running ahead. Max pulled his heavy nightstick out of his

belt. "To me, King!" he shouted, and King came hurrying back.

The shape swooped closer and Max saw that it was a bat after all — a huge, gigantic, monstrous hairy bat with sharp yellow teeth and glowing red eyes. It was coming directly at him. Max raised the nightstick above his head. As the bat swerved to avoid it, King leaped into the air and sank his teeth into one of its wings.

The bat screamed a horrible scream and began falling out of the sky. Falling with the bat, King growled deep in his throat and bravely kept his jaws clamped tightly onto the wing. The bat flailed hard with his other wing but could not get loose. It could not get back into the air. When it flopped onto the ground, King, still holding on to its wing, landed gracefully on all four feet. Max hit the bat as hard as he could with the nightstick. The bat began to shrink, melting into the grass until there was nothing left of it but a sticky, dark puddle.

"Thanks, King," Max said. "Together we have freed this world from a terrible scourge." Max liked the word *scourge*. He used it as often in his adventures as he could. He patted King on the head and King wagged his tail and licked his hand. He didn't jump up on Max and slather Max's face with slimy, smelly spit. He just licked his hand in a friendly, loyal way. *Now* this *is the way a dog ought to behave!* Max thought. He opened his eyes and imagined King lying quietly next to him on his bed. "We'll have another adventure tomorrow," Max promised. Maybe tomorrow, he thought, they'd run into a troll. A huge, gigantic mountain troll.

When he had put on his pajamas and brushed his teeth, Max went out into the living room to tell his mother good night. She was sitting in her favorite chair with a book in her lap. But she wasn't reading. She was staring out the window at the streetlight. "I don't have Goldie to walk tonight," she said, not even turning to look at him. Her voice had a weird sort of trembly sound. "I hope someone has found her. I hope whoever it is will see our signs and bring her back to us."

"Maybe," Max said.

Mother turned to him now. "I'm really sorry Polly lost your dog," she said.

"It wasn't Polly's fault," he answered. Mother didn't understand how completely true that was.

Back in his bed, Max pulled his quilt up to his chin. Didn't Mother and Polly see that they were all better off without Ratty? It might take a few days, he thought, but they'd get over this. Ali Baba probably already had. Ali Baba was probably as happy as Max was that Ratty was gone. He didn't have to run and hide under the couch anymore.

Max had left his bedroom door open a little so Ali Baba could come back and sleep on his bed again. He would very much like having Ali

Baba on his bed again, he thought. Even if sometimes he stuck a claw in Max's foot.

I'm going to stay nice and cozy and warm all night, Max told himself as he closed his eyes and snuggled into his pillow. No rat dog would pull his quilt off and leave him shivering. He could sleep later in the morning because he didn't have to walk Ratty before breakfast. He wouldn't have to apologize for her barking or jumping. Or worry about her stealing sausages. These were very, very good things. They were exactly what he had wanted — exactly!

12 **SOMETHING WAS DIFFERENT,** Max thought when he woke up. It took him a moment to figure out what it was. Then he knew. There was no warm body in his bed with him. There was no Ratty, of course. But there was no Ali Baba either. Max couldn't remember a morning when he had wakened to find himself completely alone in his bed. It felt very strange.

He looked at his clock. He hadn't slept late after all. It was the same time he had been waking up ever since Ratty came. He thought of the people who wouldn't be waving papers at him this morning or crossing the street to avoid

Ratty. Then he thought of the little old lady. Would she wonder where he was? Would she throw dog biscuits to somebody else's dog? And would that other dog be able to catch them in midair?

He fluffed his pillow, turned over, and snuggled down under his quilt. He would go back to sleep. Maybe he would have a really good dream.

But he didn't go back to sleep. His bed felt big and cold and empty. After a few minutes of keeping his eyes tightly closed and trying very hard to be asleep, he gave up and got out of bed.

On his way back from the bathroom, Max stepped on something hard and sharp. It was Ratty's rawhide chew toy. The sharp part was where Ratty had chewed the end off. *We won't be needing this anymore,* Max thought. *I can throw it away.* He put it in his sock drawer instead. He got Ratty's ball from under his desk and put it there too.

When he was dressed, Max started for the kitchen to fix himself a bowl of cereal. Polly's door was open. She was still asleep, making little wuffly sounds through her nose. Ali Baba was curled up in the crook of her legs. The cat opened one green eye and looked at Max. "Ali," Max called to him softly so he wouldn't wake Polly. "Ali! Come with me. I'll give you a treat." Ali Baba closed his eye and curled his paw around the end of his nose. Max went on to the kitchen alone.

When he had eaten his cereal and drunk a glass of orange juice, Max heard Mother's alarm go off. She would take her shower and then wake Polly, he knew. Then they would have their breakfast. It was still ages before he and Polly had to go out to the corner to meet the school bus. His homework was packed in his backpack already. There was nothing he had to do. He had never had Adventure Time in the morning. But today he could.

He went back to his room and settled himself on his bed. He closed his eyes, got quiet, and imagined himself on a narrow trail in a deep forest. King was sitting on the trail in front of him, his ears cocked, his eyes focused on Max's face. King's big plume of a tail wagged back and forth, clearing leaves from the trail as it went.

"Let's go!" Max said. He began walking along the trail. King walked next to him, keeping pace so that his dark, cold nose was right next to Max's fingers.

A squirrel ran down a tree and scurried across the trail. King just kept walking next to Max. He didn't bark. He didn't chase it. He didn't even watch the squirrel go. A fox appeared on the trail ahead of them. King ignored it. A bear came shuffling out from behind a bush. King didn't bark or even growl. Big as the bear was, King didn't even seem to notice it. "Get the bear!" Max said. Snarling, King ran toward the bear, and the bear turned and lumbered off.

As soon as it had disappeared into the forest, King came back, his tail wagging, and sat in front of Max.

Max changed the setting. Now he and King were walking along the sidewalk on 8th Avenue. King walked right next to him, ignoring the people coming and going around them. He didn't bark at other dogs, didn't chase squirrels, and didn't even look toward the window of LaRosa's. Max imagined a man walking out of the deli two doors down from LaRosa's, biting into a huge ham sandwich. King's nose didn't so much as twitch.

Max decided he wanted knights and dragons in this adventure. He imagined himself on a horse now, wearing a suit of shiny silver armor. He was back in the forest, searching for the lair of a dragon that had been roasting and eating the cattle on the farms at the edge of the forest. "Sniff out the trail," he told King. King put his nose to the ground and went ahead. When the trail branched, King sniffed to the left and then to the right. He looked back at Max and began trotting down the left-hand trail.

Soon Max saw whole, leafless branches burned black on some of the trees around him, so he knew that King had chosen correctly. After a little while, the trail curved upward and a cave entrance yawned in front of them. There were scorch marks all around its edges and bones scattered on the ground outside. Max's horse danced sideways, neighing in fright. Max reined him in. King stood his ground in front of the cave, glancing back to Max for orders.

A tongue of flame flicked from the cave's darkness. Then a dragon's head appeared, covered with shiny red scales. Its eyes were bright and bulging and burning with a greenish-yellow light.

"Ready, King!" Max said, and freed a long silver lance from its place by his saddle, readying it for combat. King growled. The dragon stepped

out into the light and unfurled its purple-and-red wings. King tensed himself to spring —

Max sighed and allowed the cave and the dragon to vanish. He knew exactly what would have happened next. King would leap at the dragon to bite its soft underbelly. The dragon would breathe fire. Ignoring the fire, King would sink his teeth into the dragon. Then Max would spur his horse, charge, and impale the dragon on his lance. He and King would have delivered the farmers of the kingdom from the

scourge of the dreaded cattle-eating dragon. They would have won, just like always.

Max turned and started back down the trail. King came with him. Max stopped. "Sit!" he told King. King sat. "Roll over!" he told King. King flopped down on the ground and rolled over. "Fly!" Max said. King jumped up. Wings sprouted from his back, just above his front legs. He leaped into the air and flew around Max's head in a big circle, in and out among the branches of the trees. There was nothing King wouldn't do for Max — nothing he *couldn't* do. But he never did anything surprising. He always did what Max wanted him to do, what Max expected or told him to do. Where was the adventure in that?

"Phooey!" Max said, and opened his eyes.

He heard Polly crying and Mother's voice coming from Polly's room. "Mrs. Chang put up lots of signs, honey," Mother was saying. "Someone will surely find Goldie. Someone will call or someone will just bring her back to us."

But Mother's voice didn't sound very reassuring. Max could tell she was only hoping to be right.

"It's all my fault!" Polly wailed.

"No, it isn't," Mother said. "You were just trying to help."

They'll get over it! Max told himself firmly again.

13

MORE THAN A WEEK PASSED with no sign of Ratty. No one called. No one brought a scruffy little yellow dog to their door. Every day, Max reminded himself of all the bad things Ratty had done to his life. He had taken his savings to LaRosa's and offered to pay for the sausage Ratty had stolen. The man had taken his money and told him not ever to bring his dog back there. That was an easy promise to make, since Ratty was gone. The trouble was, Mother and Polly weren't getting over Ratty's disappearance the way he'd expected them to.

Their father had finally called from Chicago,

where he had moved for his new job. When Polly talked to him, she didn't tell him about her nice teacher or her new friends. She talked about nothing but Ratty and how much she wanted her back.

Max was glad at first that Dad had called, but when Mother handed him the telephone, he didn't know what to say except hello. He waited for Dad to start the conversation. "Are you all broken up about this dog too?" Dad asked.

"Not like Polly," Max said. There was a long silence.

"So —" Dad said finally. "Have you made any friends at your new school?"

Max shook his head. Mother made talking signs with her fingers. "Not yet," he said.

"This is your chance to start over," Dad said. "Don't mess up. Don't just sit around daydreaming like you did before, or you'll never have any friends. Get out on the playground and mix it up. Find the toughest kid and challenge him. Tough kids respect people who challenge them."

Max didn't believe that for a minute. "Okay," he said.

"You get the tough kid on your side and everybody will want to be your friend."

"Okay," Max said again. There was another silence. "Bye," Max said and handed the phone back to his mother.

After talking for a minute or two, she said good-bye and hung up. "He just wants the best for you," she told him.

"I know." Max said it, but he wasn't sure he believed it.

Polly was crying again, and Max couldn't tell if she was crying about Ratty or about something else. Phone calls were hard, he thought. Dads were supposed to call their kids. But now he sort of wished Dad hadn't.

The next day, it rained really hard and the Lost Dog posters got all blurry. Finally somebody took them down. Polly stopped asking when the dog would come back, but after she went to bed, Max sometimes heard her crying herself to sleep. And she didn't act like herself the rest of the time. Mom said she could invite her new friends over to play, the way she used to at their old school, but she didn't. She just came home and moped around the house every afternoon. She was like a glass of soda after all the fizz is gone.

Mother sighed a lot, for no reason at all. And Max noticed how often she glanced out the window, as if she expected Ratty to show up on the stoop and bark to come in.

Ali Baba didn't run anymore, of course. Sometimes he sat on the windowsill and looked out. Mostly he just slept and ate, the way he used to. But he didn't go back to sleeping on Max's bed at night. He stayed with Polly instead. Max had to get used to sleeping by himself. He didn't sleep as much as he wanted, though. When he woke up in the morning at the time he used to walk Ratty, there was too much time before breakfast. He tried Adventure Time again, but he went alone, without King. It just wasn't much fun.

At school, Nick tripped Max twice in the hall. Max imagined rats in Nick's backpack. Rocco and Luis stole Max's backpack and broke all of his pencils. Max imagined toadstools in their sandwiches. Nick snatched Max's lunchtime banana and stomped it into a mushy mess on the playground. Max imagined a giant stomping Nick.

After that, he considered going back to Wishworks, Inc., and wishing Nick and his henchmen away the way he had wished Ratty away. It would work, he knew. And he wanted them to go away. But wishing something away was scary. So he just kept imagining rats and toadstools and giants. Imagining didn't keep the bullies from bothering him, but at least it made Max feel a little better.

When Mr. Malone talked about boring things, Max counted holes in the ceiling tiles. He watched the second hand on the clock jerk around and around. He poked holes in his note-book paper with his broken pencils.

After dinner and homework, Max used the time before bed to finish unpacking the moving boxes. He arranged all his belongings in his room just the way he wanted them. Even when he was finally finished and his room really felt like his room, he wasn't as happy as he'd hoped.

One night when Max had put on his paja-mas, he sat on his bed and thought. His life was much, much better than it used to be. He had finally stopped waking up at Ratty-walking time. He had grown used to sleeping alone in bed. Mrs. Chang had started giving him and Polly graham crackers instead of broccoli after school sometimes. And in math, Mr. Malone had started weighing and measuring, which was sort of interesting.

He and Jerome Fisher sat together on the bus all the time now. One day, Jerome had asked if he could come over and walk King with him after school. Max told him he wasn't allowed to have anybody over while his mother was at work. So Jerome invited Max to his house instead. Max got to meet Jerome's mother and his baby brother, who cried all the time. He got to stay for dinner. While they ate, Jerome's father told them more stories about his work. And before Max went home, Jerome let him feed Sam the goldfish.

But in spite of all these good things, Max wasn't happy. He had had a real dog for a while and now he didn't. An imaginary dog just wasn't good enough anymore. He couldn't have Jerome come to his house to play with King. In fact, unless he wanted to tell Jerome that King was only an imaginary dog, he couldn't have Jerome come to his house at all.

Max thought about Wishworks, Inc. He knew he could imagine himself back there any time he wanted. He knew he would always have a twenty-dollar bill in his pocket to buy another wish. And he knew that once he made the wish, it would come true.

But now he understood how tricky wishes could be. He remembered what the old man had said before his first wish: "This is the hard part." Max hadn't believed him. He hadn't thought hard enough before making that wish.

He hadn't thought hard before wishing Ratty away either. He hadn't thought how it would make Polly feel. Or Mother. Or Ali Baba. Max sighed. He hadn't even known how it would make him feel.

If he were to go back and make another wish, how would he be able to imagine all the things that might go wrong with it and keep them from happening? How could he make a wish that he could be absolutely sure would work the way he wanted it to work? And how could he really know what would make him happy before it happened?

Max took out a pad of paper and a pencil. At the top he wrote Real Live Dog. Under that he listed what he thought would make him happy:

1. The dog should like me.
2. I should like the dog.
3. It shouldn't be ugly.
4. Mother and Polly should like the dog.
5. Ali Baba should like the dog.
6. Mrs. Chang should like the dog.

Max chewed on the end of his pencil for a moment. What else?

7. The dog should be able to catch a ball in the air.
8. The dog should have a mind of its own.
9. But not so much that I can't keep it from doing awful things.

He read his list over twice. Would all those things really make him happy? *Yes,* he thought. Then he thought, *I think so.* Then he thought, *Maybe.* He was afraid something could still go wrong.

Max thought and thought and thought. And then he had an idea. He knew what he could say. It's what he should have said when he made his very first wish.

He closed his eyes and imagined himself standing in front of the counter at Wishworks, Inc. The old man smiled at him. "I figured you'd be back," he said. "It takes a while to get the hang of this."

Max nodded. He reached into his pocket and pulled out the twenty-dollar bill he knew would be there. He handed it to the old man. He said the words of his wish in his head to be sure he wouldn't make a mistake. Then he took a breath and said, "I want the *exactly right* real, live dog!"

"Done," the old man said as the cash register clanged.

14 THE SOUND OF THE CASH

register hadn't even died away before Max heard the doorbell. "I'll get it!" he yelled, leaping off his bed. He ran down the hall and reached the front door by the time his mother had gotten up from her chair. This would be his wish, he thought. It was a good wish, a *perfect* wish, and it had come true almost as soon as he made it! Outside the door already was his dog. The exactly right dog. This dog would be everything he wanted his dog to be, everything he'd put on his list. This dog would make him happy. He could feel his heart beating very fast. All he had to do was open the door and let it in.

Still, he was just a tiny bit nervous. He peered through the peephole in the door. The face of a man in a police uniform seemed to look in at him. It was Jerome Fisher's father. Maybe the right dog would be a police dog, a big, handsome German shepherd.

The moment Max opened the door, a dirty yellow blur leaped from Officer Fisher's arms and landed with a grunt and a yelp at Max's feet. Yipping and whining, it jumped up on Max, scratching his legs through his pajama bottoms. *No,* Max thought. *No, no, no, no, no!* How could the man at Wishworks, Inc., get his perfect wish so completely wrong?

Polly came running from her room, Ali Baba right behind her. "Hurray, hurray, hurray!" she was yelling. "Goldie's back!"

Max got down on his knees so Ratty couldn't

scratch his legs anymore, and pushed the dog away. She thought he was playing. She jumped at him, put her paws on his shoulders, and licked his face. Then she bounded over to Polly and flopped on her back, whining for Polly to rub her tummy.

Officer Fisher was shaking his head. "Jerome just said you knew who the dog belonged to. He didn't realize she was yours."

Ali Baba stepped out from behind Polly. The dog saw him and chased him down the hall and back again. They ran twice around the living room, and then Ali Baba went under the couch. Ratty got stuck halfway under, snarling and growling and wagging her tail furiously.

Officer Fisher introduced himself to Max's mother. She thanked him for bringing Goldie back. "Where did you find her?"

"Well, that's an odd story," he said. "I stepped out on our front stoop a little while ago and this little dog came tearing down the sidewalk. A big, reddish-brown dog was chasing her. Before I could close the door behind me, she barreled right between my legs and into the house."

Max looked up. "Did the dog that was chasing her have a big plume of a tail?"

"He sure did. Handsome dog, he was."

King! Max thought. It was the first thing King had ever done without being asked.

With a sigh, Max sat down on the floor. Ratty came over and climbed onto his lap. She was as dirty as she'd been when she first came to them. That meant he would have to give her a bath again. He groaned.

He could feel her ribs through her scruffy fur. It was a good thing they still had her food. *The* exactly right *real, live dog,* he had told the man at Wishworks, Inc. Real and live as she was, there was no way she was the right dog. No way at all.

Ratty turned around and around and lay down in his lap. Max looked at her. Something about her had changed while she was gone. Dirty as she was, she wasn't quite as ugly as she used to be. The tufts of hair around her ears didn't look so odd. Even her tail wasn't as ratty as it used to be. He touched her head. She looked up at him and blinked her eyes. He hadn't noticed before how gold her eyes were. He hadn't noticed her dark brown eyelashes. He patted her head and she reached up and licked his face again. Whatever the change was, it sure hadn't helped her breath! He wondered if there was such a thing as a doggie breath mint.

Officer Fisher was going on with his story. "As soon as the dog ran inside, I went to close the door so the big dog wouldn't follow this one in. My wife is allergic to dogs, and she was already hollering like crazy. But the big dog had just — vanished! I can't imagine where he got to. All the fuss woke the baby, of course, and he started crying. It was chaos."

Of course the big dog vanished, Max thought. He was surprised that Officer Fisher had been able to see King in the first place. No one else ever had.

"Meantime, this little dog had found Jerome and was barking and jumping all over him. Jerome said he'd seen his friend Max walking her one time."

Friend? Max thought. Jerome had called him his friend?

"He said she belonged to a family Max knew. I had to get the dog out of our house, so I thought I'd just bring her over and find out if you could tell me where she belongs."

"She belongs here," Mother said.

"I can see that!"

What, Max wondered, would he tell Jerome about King? If Jerome thought he was a friend, would he be mad that Max had lied to him?

"I didn't want Jerome to think she was my

dog," Max told Officer Fisher. "So I told him about my imaginary dog instead. His name is King."

To Max's relief, Jerome's father smiled and nodded. "Jerome used to have an imaginary dog too — name of Valiant. No allergy worries with Valiant."

Mother thanked Officer Fisher and asked if he would accept a reward for bringing Goldie back.

"No, no. I was just doing my job," he said with a grin, "taking a menace off the streets. What Jerome would call a scourge! He's heavy into fantasy. Knights and dragons and so on."

"Well, you're definitely *our* knight in shining armor," Mother said.

"Tell Jerome thanks too," Max said. "Tell him I'll see him at the bus stop in the morning." *I have a friend,* Max thought. *One who will understand about King.* The next time Dad called, Max would tell him about Jerome.

After Officer Fisher left, Mother told Max he could give Ratty a bath when he got home from school the next day. "Just be sure she sleeps on the floor tonight," she said, "so she won't mess up your bed."

As if he could make this dog do anything, Max thought. How was he going to survive having her back in his life? He thought about his chewed-up teddy bear. He thought about waking up with no covers in the night. He thought about Ratty dragging him when she chased squirrels, and having to walk her past LaRosa's. Then he remembered what the old lady had said about obedience school.

"Do you think I could take Goldie to obedience school?" he asked his mother.

She laughed. "I'd been planning to check into that very thing before she ran away. I don't think you're old enough to take her by yourself, but we could go together."

"Could I go too?" Polly asked.

"Absolutely," Mother said. "If Goldie's going to be safe with us, we all have to be able to handle her."

Also if we're *going to be safe with* her, Max thought. "Will obedience training teach her not to jump and scratch and not to chew my stuff?"

"I think the point is more to teach us how to teach her. But, Max —" Mother's voice had gotten very serious. Max looked up into her stern face. "Obedience training is going to take a lot of work. A lot of practice. You'll have to walk her more than you did before. In the morning and after school and on weekends too. You know now what it's like to have a dog. She needs you, you know. You can't just pay attention to her when you happen to feel like it. This is going to be a very big responsibility."

"I know," he said. If anybody understood how hard having Ratty was going to be, he did.

Ratty went into the kitchen and pawed at the cupboard where her food was kept. "She's hungry," Mother said.

Max got out the dog food and a bowl. Mother gave him some leftover chicken stew to spoon over the dry food. "A welcome-home treat," she said.

Ratty jumped and yelped like always, and nearly knocked the bowl out of his hands as Max put it down.

Mother made hot chocolate for Max and Polly, to celebrate. "I told you we'd get her back," she said to Polly.

They wouldn't believe how it really happened, Max thought. He watched Ratty gobble her food and lick the bowl clean. It occurred to him that he had never once thought to feed King.

15 **JEROME WAS SITTING ON HIS** camouflage sleeping bag on the floor of Max's dim and shadowy bedroom, and Max was in his bed. They were having a sleepover. It was late, but Mother had said they could stay up talking as long as they wanted. The window shade was up and the only light came from the lights of the apartment house. They each had a bowl of popcorn, and Goldie was sitting on the floor between them, watching every bite they put into their mouths.

"I don't know why you bothered with an imaginary dog when you had a real one," Jerome said. "Goldie's great. There are *dragons* whose eyes aren't as intense as this dog's."

Max nodded. "Especially when there's food around." He had said, "Goldie, sit!" and "Goldie, stay!" After nearly a month of practicing, he was mostly remembering not to call her Ratty. And after nearly a month of practicing, she was mostly remembering to sit. Right now she was quivering all over and drooling, but she wasn't jumping on them and knocking over the bowls or snatching popcorn out of their hands. *Stay* was still hard for her. He had to keep reminding her.

Ever since Goldie had begun obedience school, Max had had to walk her for fifteen minutes in the morning and half an hour after school, rain or shine. But it wasn't as bad as it might have been. Except on Mondays, when the obedience class was held, and Thursdays, when Jerome had his trumpet lesson, Jerome had mostly gone along on the training walks. Sometimes Max let Jerome hold the leash and give the commands. They pretended they were on adventures as they walked. Sometimes Goldie was a dog. Sometimes she was a tiger or a Tasmanian devil. Once they pretended she was a robot, but Jerome said a robot would obey them better than Goldie did. She was still really hard to get past LaRosa's.

On weekends, Polly and Mother and Max took Goldie to the park, where they could all take turns putting Goldie through her practice with the commands she was learning — *heel, sit, stay, come*. A lot of times, Jerome went with them. While Mother and Polly were working with Goldie, he and Max would act out adventures. Some of their adventures happened along the stream. Some happened in and around the park's stone shelters, which became whatever they needed them to be — castles or forts or bunkers.

The adventures Jerome thought up were new to Max, and Max's were new to Jerome. Sometimes the scourge the boys went after was a troll, a dragon, a giant, or a gang of goblins, and sometimes it was a bank robber or a kidnapper or a carjacker. Jerome knew more about that kind of scourge than Max did because of his father. But all the adventures were more fun with the two of them than they had ever been alone.

Jerome, who had finished his popcorn, reached under the desk to get Goldie's ball. "Let's see if she can catch this in the dark."

Goldie began barking and waggling. Jerome bounced the ball and Goldie leaped for it. She snatched it out of the air and came back down, landing gracefully on all four feet. "Air Goldie," Jerome said. "She's good!"

Max watched Jerome take the ball from Goldie and bounce it again. There had never been another kid who liked what he liked and did what he did. There had never been a kid he could invite for a sleepover.

After Jerome had bounced the ball for her three more times, Goldie dropped it and jumped onto Max's bed. Max emptied the last of his popcorn into his hand and held it out to her. She snapped it up, getting the ends of his fingers along with the popcorn. "Ouch!" he said. "Gently!" *Gently* wasn't one of the commands Goldie understood.

Jerome yawned. "Would it be okay if she slept down here with me tonight?"

"She likes to sleep on my bed." Max heard Jerome sigh as he settled down into his sleeping bag. If he put Goldie down there with Jerome, she wouldn't stay, he knew. He felt sorry that his friend had never had a pet who could share his bed.

Goldie began pawing at the quilt to make herself a place to sleep. Max moved over to give her some room. She turned around and around and then flopped down against his belly.

"That sure was a terrific adventure we had today," Max said.

"Yeah," Jerome said, and yawned again. "Terrific."

It had started in an ordinary enough way, Max thought. Jerome had been holding Goldie's leash as they walked along 8th Avenue, pretending they were time-traveling knights who had been sent to this century to save the world from the scourge of international terrorism. Goldie was their bomb-sniffing dog. They had been watching the people on the street carefully, looking for anyone who was acting strange, when they saw a woman coming out of Agatha's Antiques with a large and very oddly shaped package wrapped in brown paper. "Bomb?" Max whispered.

"Could be," Jerome whispered back.

And then, right behind the woman came Nick. He was carrying a shopping bag and clutching another brown paper package against his chest. Max had a momentary urge to hide behind a parked car. But Jerome wasn't afraid of Nick. "That's Nick's mom," Jerome said. "I bet

they're really terrorists. And both of those pack-
ages are bombs."

Nick and his mother were coming toward
them, heading for a black car parked just down
the street from the antique shop. Goldie had
stopped in the middle of the sidewalk, her nose
in the air. Her tail was circling, and a low growl
came from her throat. As they got closer, the
growl changed to a howl and she surged forward
with a lunge so fast that the leash slipped from
Jerome's hand. Dodging the feet of the other
people on the sidewalk, Goldie charged at Nick.
He saw her coming and his face seemed to go
white. Instead of holding her off with the shopping bag, Nick froze to the spot, yelling, "Dog!
Mommy, dog!"

Goldie leaped into the air and hit him a little
above the knees, knocking him backward. He
screamed as he went down onto the cement, the
brown paper package flying from his arms and

crashing down next to him with a sound of shattering glass. Goldie, the handles of the shopping bag gripped firmly in her teeth, disappeared under a delivery van parked at the curb, dragging the bag with her. As it vanished behind the van tire, Max saw LaRosa's printed on the bag.

"My vase, my beautiful vase!" Nick's mother was yelling, and Max was stunned to see that Nick, sitting on the sidewalk next to the broken package, had begun to cry. "Nicholas Humphrey Berger, look what you've done! I'll never be able to replace that vase!"

Humphrey? Max thought. *Nicholas Humphrey?*

"It wasn't me!" Nick sobbed. "It was that dog!"

"That little thing? What did you think it was going to do? Eat you?"

"You know I'm scared of dogs!" It was then that Nick caught sight of Max and Jerome. He scrubbed hurriedly at his face, as if to erase the evidence of his tears, and struggled to his feet. An old lady had come out of Agatha's Antiques with a broom in her hand. Max saw that it was the old lady who liked Goldie so much.

"Get over it," she said, in her high, thin voice. "Dogs are noble beasts. Better than a lot of humans." She began to sweep up the glass from the shattered package. "I might be able to find another vase like this one," she told Nick's mother, who was putting the other package into the backseat of their car. "Just give me a little time."

"Thank you, Agatha." Nick's mother turned back to him. "Where's the shopping bag?"

"That stupid dog got it!" he said.

"The dog got the shopping bag? You let that dog have our dinner?"

"I'll get it," Max said. He kneeled down on the curb next to the delivery van. Goldie was lying on the torn bag with half a sausage between her front paws, munching happily. He pulled the bag out from under her and held it up to Nick's mother. There were still two cheeses and a can of artichokes inside. "I'm sorry, but I think my dog ate your sausages."

"At least sausages can be replaced," she said, taking the bag from him. She shook her finger at him. "You ought to get that dog under control."

"Yes, ma'am," Max said. Jerome was grinning, and Max had to bite his lip to keep a straight face.

By the time Max managed to get Goldie out from under the delivery van, Nick and his mother had driven away and Jerome and the old woman, Agatha, had finished cleaning up the brown paper and glass. "Thank you for your help," she told Jerome. Then she reached into her pocket and pulled out a dog biscuit. "Sit!" she said to Goldie. Goldie sat. *Good dog!* She tossed the biscuit, and Goldie caught it. Agatha smiled at Max. "Obedience school?" she asked.

Max nodded.

"Very good work, young man," she said. "She may not be perfect, but you keep at it." She turned and went back into her shop, muttering as she went, "Scared of dogs — a boy as big as that!"

"That was great," Jerome said as they headed back to Max's house. "Nick Berger, scared of dogs!"

"Nicholas *Humphrey* Berger," Max said.

"You wait and see. I bet he never bothers you again!"

Max thought Jerome was probably right. He had two anti-bully weapons now — Goldie and Nick's middle name.

Jerome had switched to his knight's voice then. "Our trusty bomb-sniffing dog saved the day. She disabled those sticks of dynamite disguised as sausages."

"Indeed she did, my noble friend," Max answered. "Soon we will be able to return to our own time."

Goldie started barking at a squirrel and dragging on the leash, and Max gave her chain collar a quick jerk to distract her attention. "Sit!" he told her in his sternest voice. She sat.

"That squirrel must have had a tiny explosive implanted in its neck," Jerome said.

As they walked the rest of the way to Max's house, they had imagined what other animals a terrorist might use to plant tiny bombs around the city. "Rats and pigeons," Max said.

"Cockroaches and ants," Jerome had added.

Now Max grinned into the darkness of his bedroom. "I think today's adventure was the best one ever," he said. "Don't you?"

There was no answer. "Jerome?" he whispered.

Jerome had fallen asleep. Max looked down at the shadowy form in the camouflage sleeping bag and thought his dad had been right about one thing at least. It was good to have a friend.

He lay for a moment staring out the window at the apartment house. Every so often, the light in one of the windows blinked out. Then he imagined King, sitting next to his bed, wagging his plume of a tail. He imagined tossing him a big, juicy bone. King caught it in the air and carried it off, stepping carefully over Jerome's sleeping body and disappearing between the bookshelf and the closet. It was good to know he could still see King any time he wanted.

"Good night, Goldie," Max whispered, and scratched her gently behind the ears.

Goldie lifted her head, reached up, and licked him on the nose. Her breath, he thought, was just as terrible as ever.

STEPHANIE S. TOLAN, author of many books for children and young adults, won a Newbery Honor Medal for *Surviving the Applewhites*, and the Christopher Award for *Listen!* Also a playwright, she has, with author Katherine Paterson, adapted several well-known children's books for the stage. A passionate advocate for gifted children and the uses of imagination, she lives near Charlotte, North Carolina, with her husband, two dogs, and one cat.